FOR KATHY, BECAUSE SHE'S EVERYTHING
—P. M.

TO CATHY, GUS, AND KIM,
FAMILY WHO HAVE ALWAYS BELIEVED IN ME
—C. E.

SIMON & SCHUSTER BOOKS FOR YOUNG READERS
An imprint of Simon & Schuster Children's Publishing Division
1230 Avenue of the Americas, New York, New York 10020
Text copyright © 2010 by Peter Mandel
Illustrations copyright © 2010 by Chris Eliopoulos
SIMON & SCHUSTER BOOKS FOR YOUNG READERS is a trademark of Simon & Schuster, Inc.
For information about special discounts for bulk purchases, please contact Simon & Schuster Special
Sales at 1-866-506-1949 or business@simonandschuster.com.
The Simon & Schuster Speakers Bureau can bring authors to your live event. For more information or to
book an event, contact the Simon & Schuster Speakers Bureau
at 1-866-248-3049 or visit our website at www.simonspeakers.com.
Book design by Lucy Ruth Cummins
The text for this book is set in American Typewriter.
The illustrations for this book are rendered in watercolor.
Manufactured in China
1109 SCP
2 4 6 8 10 9 7 5 3 1
Library of Congress Cataloging-in-Publication Data
Mandel, Peter, 1957–
Bun, onion, burger / Peter Mandel ; illustrated by Chris Eliopoulos.
—1st ed.
p. cm.
Summary: Simple rhyming text follows the steps in making
and eating a tasty hamburger.
ISBN 978-1-4169-2466-1
[1. Stories in rhyme. 2. Hamburgers—Fiction.]
I. Eliopoulos, Chris, ill. II. Title.
PZ8.3.M347Bun 2009
[E]—dc22
2008000729

BUN, ONION,

BURGER

written by
peter mandel

illustrated by
chris eliopoulos

Simon & Schuster Books for Young Readers
New York   London   Toronto   Sydney

for one.

Raw . . .

rare . . .

medium . . .

well-done.

Mustard . . .

pickle . . .

mushroom . . .

swiss cheese.

Slowly ...

pouring ...

ketchup . . .

Say please!

Stacking . . .

serving . . .

spilling . . .

hot plate.

potatoes . . .

Can't wait!

Nibbling ...

biting ...

another . . .

one . . .

for you!